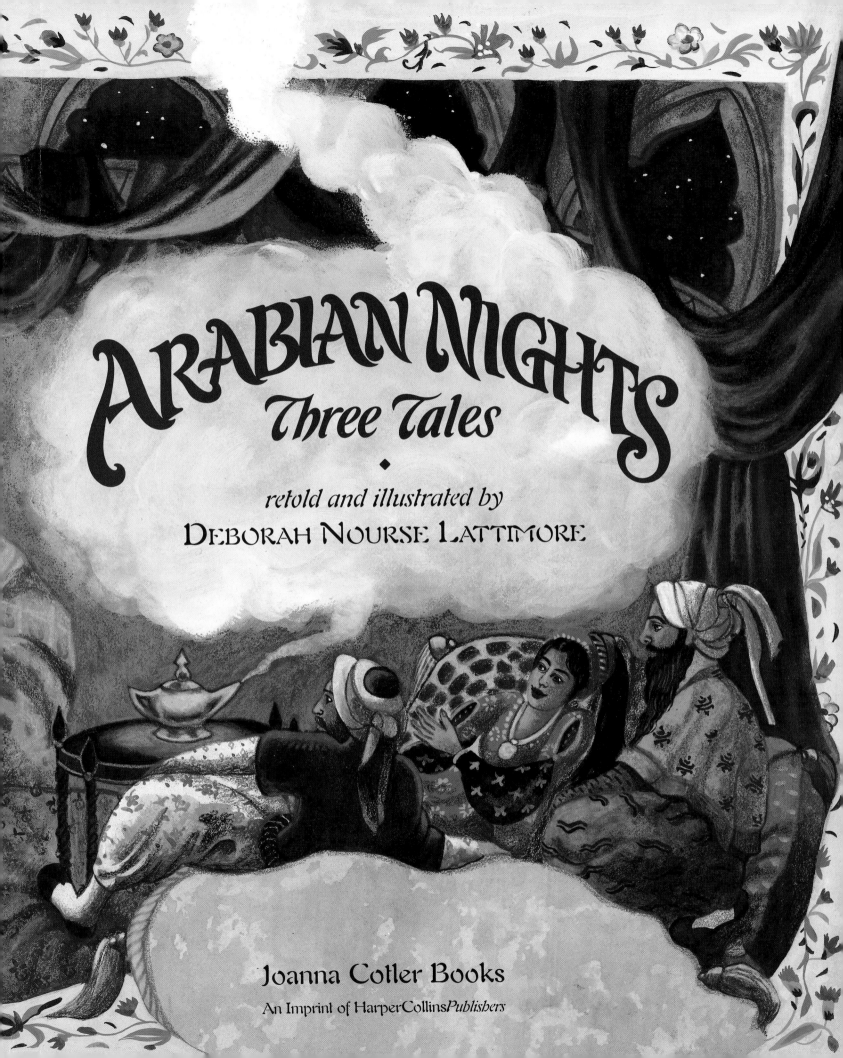

ARABIAN NIGHTS
Three Tales

•

retold and illustrated by
DEBORAH NOURSE LATTIMORE

Joanna Cotler Books
An Imprint of HarperCollins*Publishers*

Arabian Nights
Three Tales
Copyright © 1995 by Deborah Nourse Lattimore
Printed in Mexico. For information address
HarperCollins Children's Books, a division of HarperCollins Publishers,
10 East 53rd Street, New York, NY 10022.

Library of Congress Cataloging-in-Publication Data
Lattimore, Deborah Nourse.
    Arabian nights: three tales / retold and illustrated by Deborah Nourse
Lattimore.
        p.   cm.
    Summary: A retelling of three Arabian nights tales: Aladdin, The Queen
of the Serpents, and The Lost City of Ubar.
    ISBN 0-06-024585-9. — ISBN 0-06-024734-7 (lib. bdg.)
    [1. Fairy tales.   2. Folklore, Arab.]   I. Arabian nights. English.
Selections. 1995.   II. Title.
PZ8.L349Ar   1995   94-9828
398.22—dc20   CIP
                                                                     AC

Typography by Tom Starace
1   2   3   4   5   6   7   8   9   10
❖
First Edition

To Isabel and Nicholas,
and Sir Richard Burton

Author's Note

The year I was eleven, I discovered romance. I studied history and published my first story about ancient Egypt in a local newspaper. I developed a mad crush on my art teacher, and I came down with a cold that changed my life: One day, sniffling, I flopped down on my bed with Sir Richard Burton's translations of the fantastic stories Scheherazade told her husband for one thousand and one nights. Two weeks later, long after the cold was gone, I was still reading. Of all the versions I had seen of the *Arabian Nights*—some from India, others from Persia and Arabia—this one was the best. I learned that in the earliest version, the character of Aladdin had lived in old Cathay, a city on the border of China; that the real Arab word we usually see as "genie" was *jinn*; and that jinn were usually contained in fancy brass bottles called *cucurbits*. I read for hours about the Queen of the Serpents, who lived in an enchanted cave. I read about caravans with horses and camels, and of caves opening onto the Arabian Sea, where wise black men, dressed in leather, lived in mystery. On and on I read, and I always hoped that one day I would draw pictures to show what I had seen in my mind's eye.

Years later I was touring schools for the U.S. Department of Defense in Germany, and something on television transfixed me. A news flash said that Nicholas Clapp, a documentary filmmaker, had actually discovered Ubar, the lost City of Brass the fictional Scheherazade had described in the *Arabian Nights*.

Mr. Clapp had seen a silvery line, visible only on a satellite photograph, that he felt sure was the well-worn trace of the old caravan trade route, trod for centuries by merchants carrying valuable frankincense from Ubar to other cities. Research and archaeological digging revealed Ubar had been a prosperous city from around 5,000 years ago until sometime between A.D. 200 and 400, when the entire city completely collapsed, dropped into the sand, and disappeared into a subterranean sinkhole far below the ground line. Not only did Nicholas Clapp find the city, which until then had been thought to be mythical; he also found Scheherazade's mysterious caves where wise black men lived, and the very caravan trails I'd read about years before.

I knew Nicholas Clapp had found the most remarkable link between myth, folktale, and real life. I was able to contact Mr. Clapp, and in him found someone who felt as excited and enthusiastic about ancient history as I did, if not more so. What a stroke of luck! It was as if we had been able to step back through the veil of myth and time itself and become one with Ubar, to see Scheherazade's story as fact and not fiction. Amazing!

Of all the stories I might have chosen from the *Arabian Nights*—and after all, there are enough of them to entertain a Sultan for one thousand and one nights—I chose three that meant something special to me: "Aladdin," because the story shows that even if a person has a slow start in life, he or she can triumph one day; "The Queen of the Serpents," because of the Queen's compassion and knowledge and the passing of wisdom from one generation to the next; and "Ubar, The Lost City of Brass," because Ubar lives again through the work of Nicholas Clapp and, above all, because the discovery of Ubar makes me wonder: Maybe those old, old stories aren't just make-believe after all!

D.N.L.

Aladdin

There once lived in ancient Cathay a youth, the son of a tailor, called Aladdin. While his widowed mother spun yarn all day to trade for their food, Aladdin spent all his time with the urchins of the city playing knucklebones. For all his good looks and truthful nature, Aladdin had no equal in his laziness.

One day, there appeared in the midst of the bazaar a tall, lean stranger. Dressed in the cloth of Morocco, he had the appearance of a Darwish, a Magician. Now this fellow walked up and down the streets until he spied Aladdin and, inquiring after him, discovered he was the most honest boy among the urchins. Thereupon the Magician ran up to Aladdin, embraced him, and weeping said:

"Oh, thou, Aladdin! Son of my late brother, the tailor! I am your long-lost uncle. Take me to your dear mother, that I may increase your fortune!"

With that he pressed ten gold dinars into Aladdin's hands and kissed him roundly on both cheeks, quite amazing all who watched, none more than Aladdin himself. Straightaway Aladdin took him to his mother's house, so glad was he to have a newfound uncle.

"How can it be that my poor husband had a brother but never told me?" asked the widow.

But the Magician wept and told such sweet stories that finally they made him welcome. That evening, the Magician's servants appeared with trays laden with fruits and sweetmeats and goblets brimming full. Aladdin and his mother supped as never before, and the three of them visited well into the night.

The next morning the Magician arrived at their house with his arms open wide. "Come, lad," he said to Aladdin. "I will buy you new clothes and set you up in a shop of your own, that you may make your way in this world."

Now even though the newfound uncle pressed more gold dinars into the widow's hands, she felt uneasy and would not have let her son go off with this fellow but that they needed the money so badly. And so she bade Aladdin go.

Aladdin and the Magician strolled through the marketplace together, first stopping to buy new clothes for the youth, next to purchase goods and then a shop.

After some time, the Magician smiled and said, "This city dust is upon me, and I would go with you for a walk beyond the gates to admire the gardens and trees."

Aladdin, not wishing to annoy his new uncle, agreed to go. But he wondered what gardens he might mean. For beyond the city was nothing but desert and rocky mountains. Still, they went.

After a good two hours' walk, the Magician sat down upon a rock and fanned himself. Aladdin looked back toward home and, seeing the sun go down, said, "Uncle, it is the sunset hour, and soon it will be difficult to see our way back if we do not leave now."

"Aladdin," said the Magician, "you, with your honest face. If you do my bidding, you will become the richest of the rich. Now, go and fetch me some twigs and wood chips and anything that will burn, and you shall behold a wondrous sight!"

Aladdin looked at the Magician, whose face now shimmered with an eerie light, and his legs began to tremble. But something in the Magician's eyes made him go and do as he was told.

When the woodpile was ready, the Magician stood over it and took a small box from his sleeve, opened it, and poured a fine, black powder onto the wood. Muttering loudly a string of strange incantations, he set fire to it. A burst of fire, coal, and ash rose like a whirlwind from the place, and the ground split open with the thunder of the Emperor's army. Before them, leading down into the bowels of the earth, was a polished marble staircase, agleam in the moonlight.

"Now, son of my brother," said the Magician, "wear my ring and no evil will befall you." And he put the ring on Aladdin's finger. "Go down these stairs and see for yourself the Treasure of a Thousand Jinn. At the foot of the stairs you will find four chambers: the first of precious metals, the second of precious jewels, the third of precious vessels and plates and goblets, and the fourth a garden of delights. Find the lamp that lights the place. Take it, and after you pour off the oil, put it in your belt and bring it up to me. But take care! Touch nothing else, not with your hand nor with the hem of your clothes, or the place will close up!"

Aladdin shook terribly at the edge of the stairs. He looked down and could not move. But the Magician, towering behind him, put his long, bony hand on Aladdin's back and shoved him in.

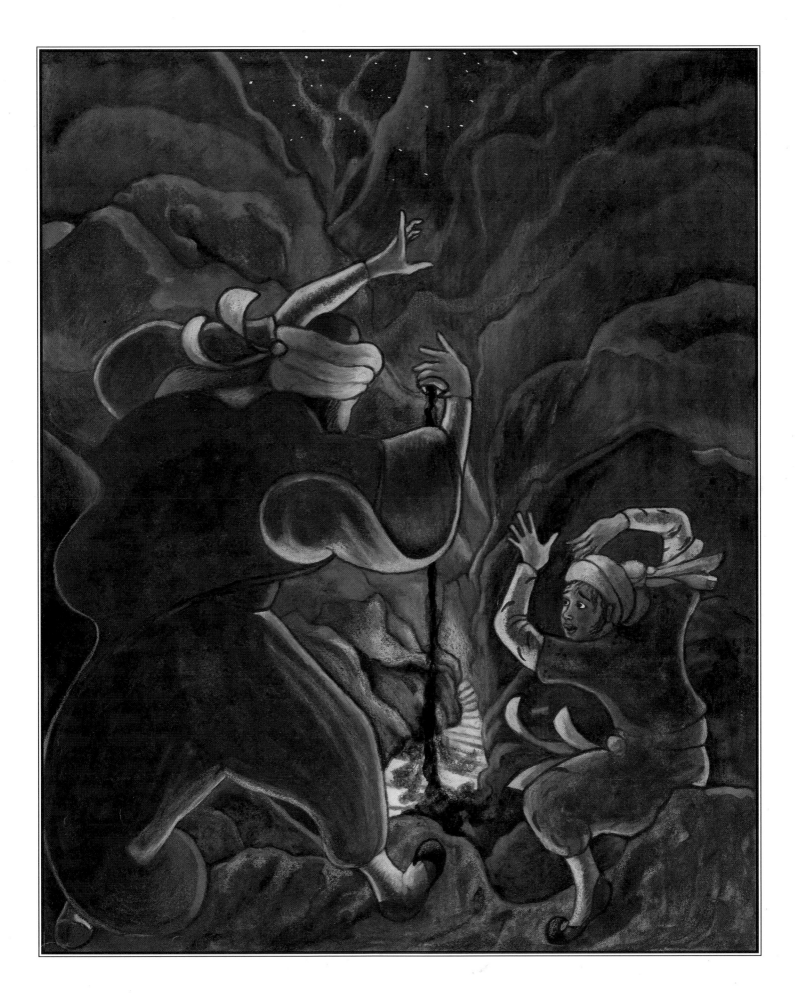

Down the marble stairs went Aladdin, one foot before the other, his eyes wide with the wonder of the place. He found everything as his uncle had told him, and when at last he reached the fourth chamber, Aladdin saw an old brass lamp hanging from a golden tree branch. Carefully he took it down, poured off the oil, and tucked it into his belt.

"Did you find the lamp?" called out the Magician.

"Yes, Uncle," replied Aladdin.

"Then come quickly, quickly!"

Aladdin started to go, but he felt his belly rumbling.

"I'll just take a few of these fruits. Surely they are of no value except to eat thereof," he said to himself, for he did not know they were fruits of precious jewels. He plucked a few from each branch, stuffing them into the deep pockets of his new clothes.

"Hurry, my brother's son!" yelled the Magician. "The magic is waning fast!"

Aladdin made for the stairs without further delay, but the rooms behind him murmured and groaned as if to shut themselves up behind him, and the marble staircase began to quake.

"Uncle!" he cried. "Give me your hand! The stairs are sinking!"

"I cannot reach so far," called back the Magician. "Throw me the lamp!"

"Please, Uncle," Aladdin returned. "Help me!"

"Ah, you fool!" yelled the Magician. "You must have touched something, or this would not have happened. Throw me the lamp now, you son of all great idiots!"

And as Aladdin tripped on his own hem and the window to the sky

shrank before his eyes, he saw the Magician swearing and cursing above him. Aladdin felt the dirt fall down upon him, and as he swept his hand over his face, Aladdin looked up and saw a different, devilish face glaring down at him, all fire and flames, and the place sealed itself over his head with a deafening crash.

Aladdin looked around him. In the dim light he could tell that there was no escape.

"Oh, if only I had spent my time in better ways!" he moaned. And he thought of how idle he had been, of his poor mother left without any family, and of how differently he would live if he were free. And as he sat, Aladdin wrung his hands in despair. Suddenly, without any warning, a beam of blue light shot out from the ring on his hand and a Jinn stood before him.

"What?" cried Aladdin. "Who are you?"

"I am the Jinn of the Ring," said the Jinn. "Your wish is my command."

Aladdin took no time in wondering. He had realized the minute the Magician had closed up the hole that he was not his uncle but an evil Sorcerer, and he understood at once the power of his ring.

"Take me to my home, Jinn!"

And no sooner had he said it than Aladdin was transported to his house and carefully set down right in front of his mother.

"My son! My son!" the widow cried, and embraced Aladdin.

When Aladdin told her of his adventure, he again summoned the Jinn of the Ring and asked for food and drink. And while they ate, the widow looked at the lamp tucked in her son's belt.

"What is that lamp you have?" she asked.

"Not much, I think, Mother, except that the Magician wanted it."

"Perhaps if I clean it, it will fetch some money in the bazaar," she replied.

Aladdin rubbed the lamp to see how dirty it was. Suddenly a great gust of smoke shot out, and there stood a Jinn even greater than the Jinn of the Ring.

"Command and I obey!" he said with a thundering voice. "I am the Jinn of the Lamp."

Aladdin bade him bring more food, and every day thereafter for a week he and his mother ate well. Aladdin was considering what to do next when there was a noisy racket on the street outside.

"What is happening, Mother?" Aladdin asked.

"Today is the day the Emperor's daughter comes from her childhood home to live in the great palace. All the city's inhabitants must close up their windows and stay inside, because it is forbidden to look upon her face."

With that the widow closed the windows. But when she turned her back, Aladdin peeked through the blinds, and in the instant that he spied the Princess, he fell in love with her.

"Mother!" cried Aladdin. "I saw the Princess! You must go to the palace and take these fruits from the cavern, give them to the Emperor, and tell him that I wish to ask for his daughter's hand in marriage."

The widow was quite astounded by what her son said, but he would not stop pleading, day or night. At last she took the jeweled fruits and went to the palace.

The Emperor was amazed at the sight of the fruits, but as he looked at the poor widow in her ragged clothes, he laughed and said, "Yes, tell this

poor woman her son may marry my daughter just as soon as he builds a palace for her in the Imperial Gardens!" And he laughed again at the thought of it.

No sooner had the widow told Aladdin this than he called forth the Jinn of the Lamp and commanded him to build in the Imperial Gardens the finest palace in the world. Then Aladdin commanded the Jinn to dress him and his mother in cloth of silk and gold, and have them transported at once to the Emperor's palace.

At the sight of them, the Emperor fell back on his throne in wonderment. The Princess, who had seen Aladdin from her window, had fallen in love with him at first sight. She begged her father to have the royal wedding the next day and did not leave off begging and sighing until the Emperor could see that there was nothing else to do. And so the next day Aladdin and the Princess were wed with all the population celebrating in great merriment.

Now everything would have been fine except that the evil Magician had returned to Cathay from his home in Morocco. When he heard that a strange new Prince had married the Princess and had built a fine palace in just one day, he knew instantly that it must be the work of a Jinn and that Aladdin must have kept his lamp. So he dressed as a seller of lamps and strolled beneath the walls and towers of the new palace crying, "New lamps for old! New lamps for old!"

It so happened that the Princess heard him calling out and, spying the old brass lamp, willingly traded it to the Magician for a shiny new one. "My Prince Aladdin will be so pleased that I have replaced this old tarnished lamp!" she said to herself.

But the minute the Magician held the lamp in his hand, he called up the Jinn and commanded him to move the palace and the Princess to his home in faraway Morocco. That night, when Aladdin returned to the Imperial Gardens, he was shocked to find his bride and his home missing.

"There is no power on earth save that of the evil Magician that could work this deed!" he moaned. And Aladdin began to wring his hands in despair once again. And just as quickly as before, the Jinn of the Ring appeared.

"Command and I obey, O Master," he said.

"Bring me my palace and my wife!" shouted Aladdin.

But alas, the Jinn only shook his head and said, "This I cannot do, for it is the spell of the Jinn of the Lamp."

"Then take me to my bride, wherever she may be!" commanded Aladdin.

In the blink of an eye, Aladdin found himself in Morocco, standing before his own home. He stole into the palace and found his bride. Together they plotted to put a sleeping potion into the Magician's wine. They watched and waited, and sure enough, the Magician drank the wine and fell into a deep sleep.

Aladdin rubbed the ring, and when the Jinn appeared, he said, "O Jinn of the Ring, send this evil Magician far away so that he never returns! If you do this, I shall set you free forever!"

"I hear and obey!" said the Jinn, laughing. "When I am gone, throw down the ring and break it, and I shall truly be free!"

And as soon as the Magician vanished from view, and indeed from the face of the earth, Aladdin threw down the ring and broke it.

Then he picked up the lamp and, rubbing it, said, "O Jinn of the Lamp! Take us back at once to the Imperial Gardens and restore us to our former happiness, and I shall set you free!"

"I hear and obey," said the Jinn of the Lamp.

And in an instant the palace was restored to its former place in the Imperial Gardens, and Aladdin and his bride lived there forever. And no one saw the evil Magician again, nor a Jinn, either!

The Queen
of the Serpents

There was once a truly wise man of Greece named Daniel the Sage, whose learning and knowledge helped friends and scholars alike. Every night he prayed for a son who could inherit his great library. As the Heavens have ears and listen to the prayers of the good, his wish was granted and his wife soon bore a fine son.

Now it chanced that Daniel was called away on a sea voyage, and with him he took all his treasured books. A terrible storm arose and turned the ship over. It was only by rare fortune that Daniel was saved, the only one, by hanging on to a wooden plank. He returned home ill with only five books left. To his wife he said, "Keep these books safe, and one day, when our son is old enough, give them to him." And the poor man died.

Daniel's wife called in an astrologer to chart the future of her son. "O woman," said the astrologer, "this son of thine will face many perils, but if he lives through them, he shall be wise indeed."

As Hasib grew up, he was little like his father. He did not work nor go to school, nor was he useful to his mother. One night the widow cried aloud to the neighbors, "Oh, for my husband! If only my son were half so wise!"

And the neighbors said, "Get him an ass, some cords, and an ax and let him join the woodcutters. Then at least he shall be useful."

So Hasib joined the woodcutters and every day went to the forests and every night sold wood in the village. One day a violent storm broke over the woodcutters' heads, and they found shelter in a cave. While he waited for the clouds to break, Hasib absentmindedly struck at the dirt floor with his ax. "Behold!" he cried out. "I have struck something!" He cleared away the earth and found a flagstone with a ringed handle. Then, calling his comrades, Hasib took hold of the ring and pulled the flagstone up. What did they find but a cistern filled with golden honey. Then and there they decided to dig it up and sell the honey for great fortune. But the woodcutters did not want to share their money, so they pushed Hasib down the cistern and dragged the flagstone over him. His mother was told that he had disappeared, and she wept herself to sleep.

Meanwhile, Hasib felt his way along the walls in the darkness until he came to a crevice. He worked at it with his fingers until he opened a window to a gleaming corridor all of silver.

Hasib followed the path of silver past a shining lake and up a small hill, upon which was a golden throne. Overcome with fatigue, he sank down and slept. Before long he awakened to the sounds of hissing and snorting. What he had thought was a lake of shimmering water was instead a sea of serpents! As Hasib counted his last minutes, watching the serpents' eyes burning at him brighter than coals, along came a snake bigger than a horse, bearing a huge golden tray upon which was another serpent, shining like crystal, with the face of a woman!

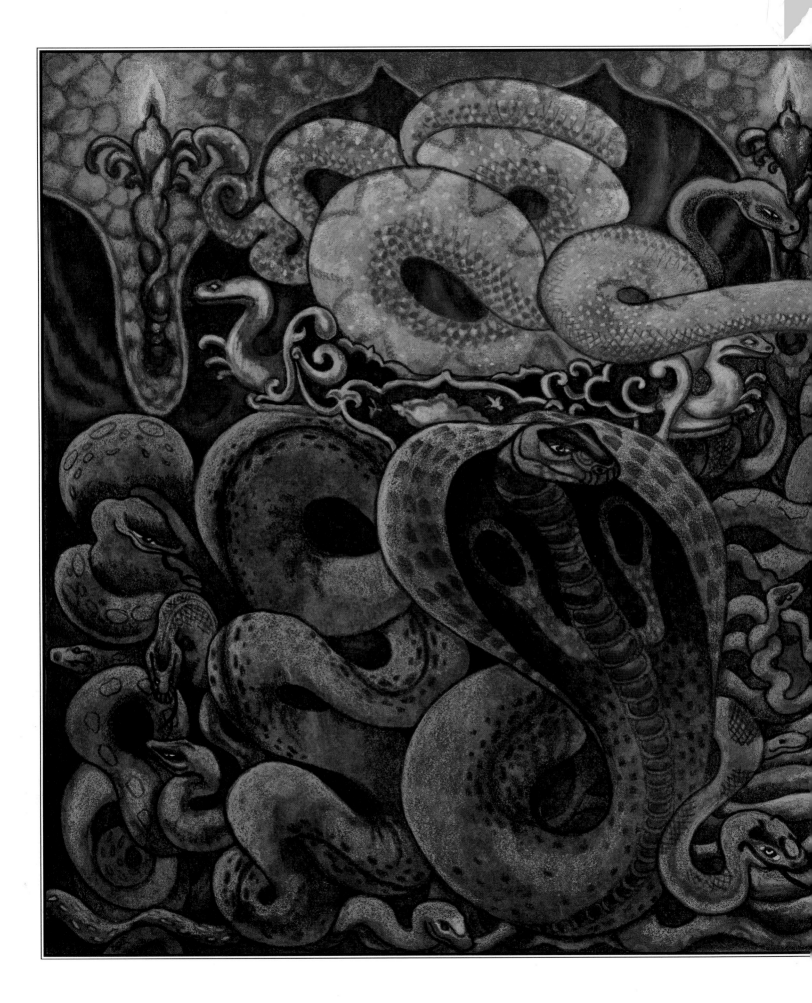

She slid down onto a golden throne beside Hasib and said, "Have no fear! I am the Queen of the Serpents and I welcome you hither. Your coming was ordained long ago."

So they dined on food and drink rare and lush, and the Queen entreated Hasib to stay with her. Back and forth they told each other stories until two years had passed and Hasib found himself knowing a wonderment of tales.

But at last Hasib longed for his home and wept to the Queen of the Serpents to let him go. This saddened the Queen, but after some time she said, "You may go as long as you swear an oath never to bathe at the hammam, the bathhouse, in your village."

Hasib swore his oath to her, and then she led him to an abandoned well that opened onto an old road leading into his village.

Hasib made his way home, and when he knocked on his mother's door, she came weeping with joy at the sight of him. She took him to the woodcutters and said, "Look you, for my son lives! What of his share of your fortune?"

The woodcutters were ashamed, so they saluted Hasib and gave him goods and shops and houses and all the wealth of his heart.

Now Hasib, with his wealth and the knowledge from the Queen of the Serpents, became a much-loved man and chief of the guild. One day a bathman at the hammam called out to him to come in and be washed by way of their hospitality. But Hasib remembered his oath to the Queen, and said no. The bathman asked a second time, and likewise Hasib said no. The third time, the bathman and his servants laughingly dragged him into the bath, pulled off his clothes, and began to wash him, and all before Hasib could stop them.

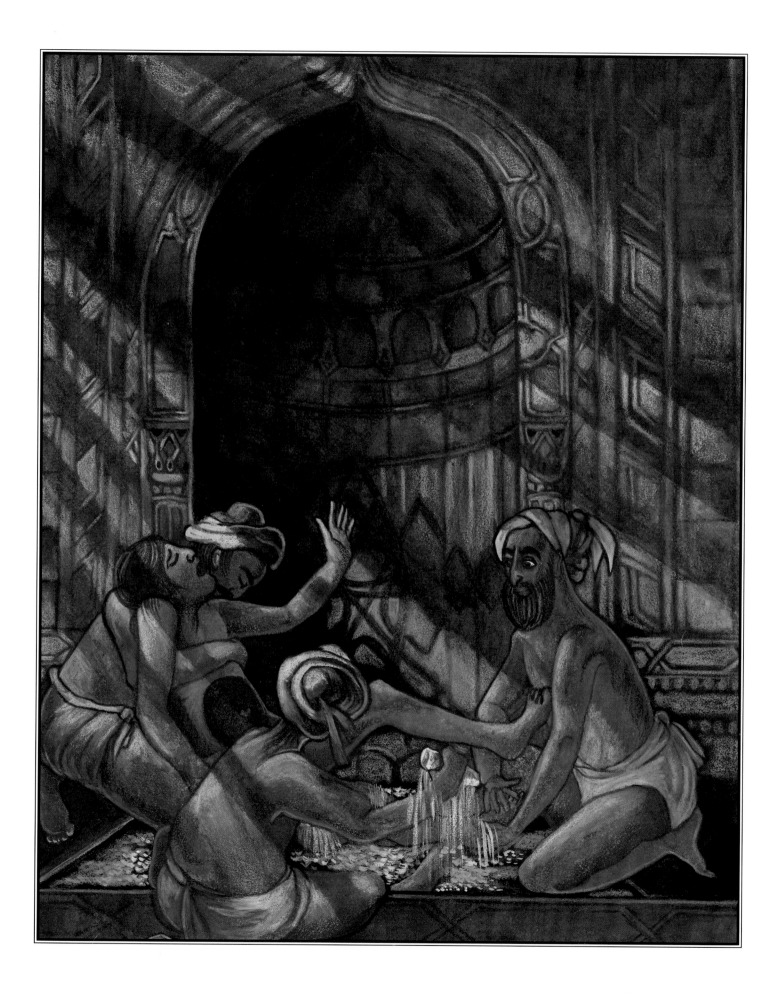

Suddenly the hands of a dozen men were upon him. Hasib found himself forced to the Sultan's palace. There the Sultan's Minister gave him drink and food and garments of honor and said to him, "Our astrologers say that you alone can save our Sultan, who is even now near death."

"Indeed!" replied Hasib. "If I knew how to save the Sultan, I would. But I know nothing of medicine!"

"But you are the one!" answered the Minister. "The astrologers said that a man who had seen the Queen of the Serpents would have the cure, and we would know him as a man whose belly turned black when he washed in the hammam. You are that man!" And Hasib looked down and saw that his belly had indeed turned black.

But Hasib denied knowing the Queen of the Serpents. Finally the Minister sent Hasib to be beaten until he could take no more, and thereupon Hasib led the Minister and his guards to the old well. The Minister stood over it muttering formulas and casting spells. Soon the water sank away and a door opened and a thunderous sound came from inside. Everyone sank to his knees in dreadful fear. Out came a serpent bigger than an elephant, carrying the golden tray, and on it was the Queen of the Serpents. She looked around and, seeing Hasib, called out, "You have broken your oath to me! Ah! But this too was written, and so I place no blame on you, Hasib."

And she began to weep and Hasib, too, wept bitterly at the sight of her. The wicked Minister reached out to take hold of her, but the Queen said, "Hold back your hand or I will turn you to ashes!" Then she said, "Hasib and no other shall carry me."

So, with the golden tray on his head, Hasib followed the Minister and his men back toward the palace.

"Hasib, listen now to me," said the Queen of the Serpents. "I know this Minister to be evil, and so you must carefully do as I say. First he will tell you to kill me, but you must tell *him* to do it. Then he will tell you to cut my body up into three parts and boil them and then draw off three potions from the brew. He will ask you to drink the first phial and to give him the second two. Beware! Give him the first one, drink the second one, and save the last for the Sultan."

When they had reached the palace, the Minister told Hasib to kill the Queen, but Hasib could only weep and turn away.

"How can you weep for nothing but a giant worm?" said the Minister, and he cut the serpent into three pieces and cast them in a pot.

"While I am away in the palace, draw up three phials. Drink the first one and save the others for me."

Hasib drew off the potions and, remembering the Queen's words, drank the second phial and saved the others.

"How do you feel?" asked the Minister when he returned.

"I burn from head to toe," answered Hasib, still weeping after the Queen.

"Fool!" laughed the Minister. "Give me the second phial." No sooner had he put down the glass Hasib presented than he fell down dead. Hasib saw that this would have been his own fate had the Queen of the Serpents not warned him.

Hasib made his way to the Sultan, the third phial cradled in his hands.

"Drink of this potion and be cured," he said to the Sultan.

Night passed to day and the Sultan was, indeed, cured. And Hasib told him how his Minister had wanted to kill him and would have succeeded if the Queen of the Serpents had not warned him.

"Ah," sighed the Sultan, "I wonder how long it would have been before my own Minister killed me, too, if murder was in his heart."

The two of them talked far into the night, and it became clear that Hasib, through his two years with the Serpent Queen and by virtue of the magical potion, was the wisest man on earth. And when Hasib's mother was called to the palace, she brought with her Daniel's last five books, and as Hasib read them, he saw that everything the Queen had told him was true and he forever praised her memory.

Ubar,
The Lost City
of Brass

It has been related in many years gone by that once there was a Caliph of Damascus who loved to gather his court around him to hear stories of even longer ago. His favorite storyteller was Talib, who one night told a wonderful tale of Solomon, son of David.

"And the power God gave Solomon over birds and beasts and all other creatures he also gave to him over the Jinn, especially evil Jinn."

"What did he do with them?" asked the Caliph.

"Why, Lord," said Talib, "he put them in copper cucurbits, or bottles, stopped them up with melted lead, and sealed the tops with his ring. These bottles were thrown far out to sea. Sometimes a fisherman catches one and opens it, and the Jinn, thinking Solomon is still alive, says, 'I repent! Never again shall I ever do a wicked deed!' and flies away."

The Caliph sat with his hand holding his beard, thinking.

"I wish I could see one of these bottles! I wish I could hold one in my hand!"

"Well, Lord," replied Talib, "if one could find the City of Brass, one could also find the sea beyond it. That is where Solomon threw the bottles."

"Aha!" cried out the Caliph. "Go for me at once! I will spare you no men, nor gold, nor provisions for your travels. But pray, find this place and return with even one of these bottles!"

"I hear and I obey!" said Talib, and he went to make ready his caravan.

The next morning, the Caliph bade Talib go by way of the desert between Damascus and Egypt and meet his cousin, Emir Musa. He gave Talib a letter asking that the Emir join the caravan with his cavalry, for no one could tell what dangers they might meet.

It was not long before Talib reached Emir Musa, and when Musa read the Caliph's letter, he embraced Talib as a brother and they discussed which way to travel. But since neither of them had ever traveled that far away, they called in the Shakir, Emir Musa's wise man.

"How long will we travel?" asked Emir Musa.

"It is a journey of four months, perhaps more," said the Shakir. "Please let me go with you so I may write down all the wonders we see, that others may read of them."

And so Talib the storyteller, Emir Musa the powerful ruler, and Shakir the wise man set out on the road with a great caravan of two thousand cavalry, and each and every one had food and drink in juglets that would not dry up in even the worst desert winds.

Through ruins of cities where desert sands blow, and beyond wastelands thirsty for all time, they traveled for one whole year.

"Great Emir!" cried Talib. "I fear greatly we are lost!"

To this Emir Musa nodded his head in worry. But the Shakir held aloft his hands to the Heavens and said, "Praise Allah and throw away greed and evil, and we shall find our way!"

With that they again set out. The next day they came to a fair and level place as smooth as a calm sea. At the edge, where the eye can see the land no more, there arose suddenly a high castle! Black stone it was and gruesome, like a dark, towering mountain, with frowning towers and an immense door of dazzling China steel.

"What means this, wise Shakir?" asked Musa.

"It is the first warning," said the old man.

"Then we should go back!" said Talib, his knees shaking fearfully.

"No, friend," said the Shakir, smiling. "A warning is simply a warning. If we pay attention to it, we shall continue our great adventure. For how is it that an entire City of Brass be lost except that all its people did something wrong in the eyes of Allah? And if we praise Allah and throw away any ill feelings of our own, how can we fail but to find this place that until now was known only in stories? So I say to you, this place will tell us many things."

Musa and Talib and the Shakir went up to the gate and found before it a pavilion with eight doors of sandalwood studded with nails of gold and stars of silver. Before it was a tablet, and the Shakir read it aloud:

"No matter how mighty these walls may seem to your eyes, remember that all who once here breathed are now gone. All they lived for was dinar upon dinar; greed fathered greed. Know thou that I, the son of a King, am buried here and all my wicked ways died with me. If you would fare on, be of a good spirit. O thou! Remember me!"

All this the Shakir wrote down, and Emir Musa wept for the lost King and all his people, too, and Talib thought of the stories he would tell.

In three days' time the great caravan went up a rocky hill, and on the top was a magnificent horseman of brass. High in the air he held a spear upon which was written:

If you come to me looking for the City of Brass, rub my hand and I shall point the way.

Talib rubbed the brass horseman's hand, and the statue spun around and around and then stopped, pointing in a direction completely different from the one they had been traveling toward. This worried the Emir and Talib, but the Shakir reassured them, and so they went on.

In three more days they came to an enormous pillar of black stone, like a giant chimney reaching up into the sky. In its center was a huge and terrible Afreet, a wicked Jinn, buried up to his chest. He had brilliant black skin, a pair of wings, two human arms, and two arms like a lion's with claws of steel. His hair was like a horse's tail and his eyes were slits with burning coals in them. But worst of all was a third eye shooting fire and smoke! The caravan drew back, every man among them shaking.

"Glory to Allah!" cried out the frightful Afreet. "Glory to all good men. Come closer and I will tell you how I came to be in this pillar. I will not harm you. By the will of Solomon I must forever be buried here."

With that the Shakir brought Emir Musa and Talib closer, and sitting before the Afreet, they awaited his words.

"I was once a great evil and wicked force on this earth," said the Afreet.

"I waged war against all good men and loved it. I gave a temple idol of carnelian to the King's daughter, but I lived in it and told her evil things to do, most awful things of which I cannot speak. Solomon warned me and all my kind, but I only laughed in his face. With his dread vengeance Lord Solomon slew my men, except for some Jinn he put into brass cucurbits stopped with lead, which he threw into the sea. As for me? I am left here, a warning to all who pass by."

Talib and Musa and the Shakir were greatly moved by these words and quietly thought of all the Afreet had said.

"I know why you have come," said the Afreet. "You will find your City of Brass on this road, a path of sand like silk, soon to be lost for all time. Go, quickly, and Allah be with you!"

The caravan moved on. For days and nights it traveled until it reached a wall of blackness and two towering bonfires. And although they were sorely frightened, Talib, Musa, and the Shakir approached and saw that the black wall was another gate of China steel and the bonfires were towers and pillars all of brass, glittering in the sunlight. There, before them, was the City of Brass, not seen by man or beast for hundreds of years!

At every wall was a tablet warning them to do only good deeds and think only good thoughts. Talib memorized them, the Shakir wrote them down, and the Emir sent a man to look for an entrance to the city. But nowhere was there an entrance. So Musa ordered his men to build a ladder at once.

When the ladder was ready, a soldier was sent up to the highest tower to look in. When he reached the top of the wall, he stood with arms outstretched and yelled aloud, "How beautiful!" Then he fell below to his death on the other side. Musa sent a second soldier up the ladder, and he too stood at the top, stretched out his arms and yelled, "How beautiful!" and toppled off the wall. A third and then a fourth and a fifth climbed up, and soon a dozen had gone up and a dozen had fallen.

"No more shall climb this terrible place!" said Musa. "Something awful must be on the other side, something frightening and evil!"

"Then I shall go," said the Shakir. "I am your wise man, and if I cannot do it, no one else can."

"But if anything happens to you, we will all be lost," said Musa. "Please, do not go."

But the Shakir went up even though Musa begged him not to. And when the Shakir reached the top of the wall, he called out the words he had copied from the tablets, warnings against evil and prayers for the good. He looked around him and then called down to Musa and Talib, "I am all right! I chased away ten fiery maidens who beckoned me to them. As soon as I spoke, they flew away!"

With that the old man walked along the walls until he came to the two brass towers and saw, just beneath them, another horseman all of brass. A message written on his hand said to turn a pin in his belly and the great gates would open. This the Shakir did twelve times. With blasts of thunder and lightning, the horseman turned around and around and shots of brasslike fire exploded from the ancient hinges of the gate until the city was open to all.

Musa and Talib and half the cavalry slowly entered the silent City of Brass. Before them was an incredible sight. Everywhere they looked, the people of the town were still and lifeless as if asleep, but were dead. The chamberlains, the guards, the officers of the court, all lay upon silken couches in their finest robes and not one of them moved. Talib and Musa and the wise man entered the marketplace, and here, too, all were dead. Around them was the greatest silk market they had ever seen, with brocades and gowns and carpets richer than eyes could imagine or hands touch. And in the apothecaries' shops were piles of ambergris and perfumes and medicines from all around the world and vessels of ivory and gold, none of them touched for hundreds of years!

On and on they walked, until they came to a palace lined with banners and hung with gold swords and bucklers and helmets lined with red gold. The vestibules were strewn with ivory couches, and the walls were of the deepest lapis lazuli. Ahead of them was a jetting alabaster fountain. Behind that was a pavilion.

"The floor!" cried Talib, slipping.

Musa rushed up to him, and he too fell. The Shakir helped them up, and the three of them wondered as they looked down. The floor leading to the pavilion seemed to be wet, as if a wild river were rushing by, but it was an illusion: Deep set into the floor were brilliant mosaic tiles waving and wandering as water wants to do, but it seemed so real that it was all they could do to shut their eyes lest they be carried away by the flow of water.

"Scatter sand here, quickly," called out the Shakir. Talib and Musa did this, and the three of them continued, their hearts beating fiercely.

The pavilion stood before them. It was held up on columns of ivory and alabaster and inlaid with every precious jewel possible. Its dome was red gold, with lattice windows jeweled with rods of emeralds. And in the center of the pavilion was a couch, and on that couch lay a damsel guarded by two soldiers, one black, one white, both made of Andalusian copper.

"Look at her eyes!" whispered Musa. "They see us!"

"No, Musa," said the Shakir. And Talib saw that though her eyelashes moved in the afternoon breeze, and her eyes were open wide, the damsel was still for all time.

"Here! I shall read this tablet aloud," said the Shakir.

"Fear this place, O ye who come, for you are the last living souls to see me and my palace and my City of Brass. Beware our greedy and evil ways, for it was our greed that brought us to our doom and my love of riches of the earth that brought down all our people for eternity. Take what you will and leave. But touch not my jewels, for I am destined to wear them in my timeless death."

Musa and Talib and the Shakir directed their men to take some of the brocades and silks and pack them quickly, for even as they stood in the courtyard, the ground began to shiver as if an earthquake were about to happen. When all the camels were laden, the three of them bade good-bye to the Queen of the City of Brass and turned to go. But a soldier walked up to the couch and said, "Why should we leave the jewels here? The dead have no use for them!"

No sooner had his fingers touched her crown than one of the Queen's copper guards drew down his brass sword and cut off the soldier's head.

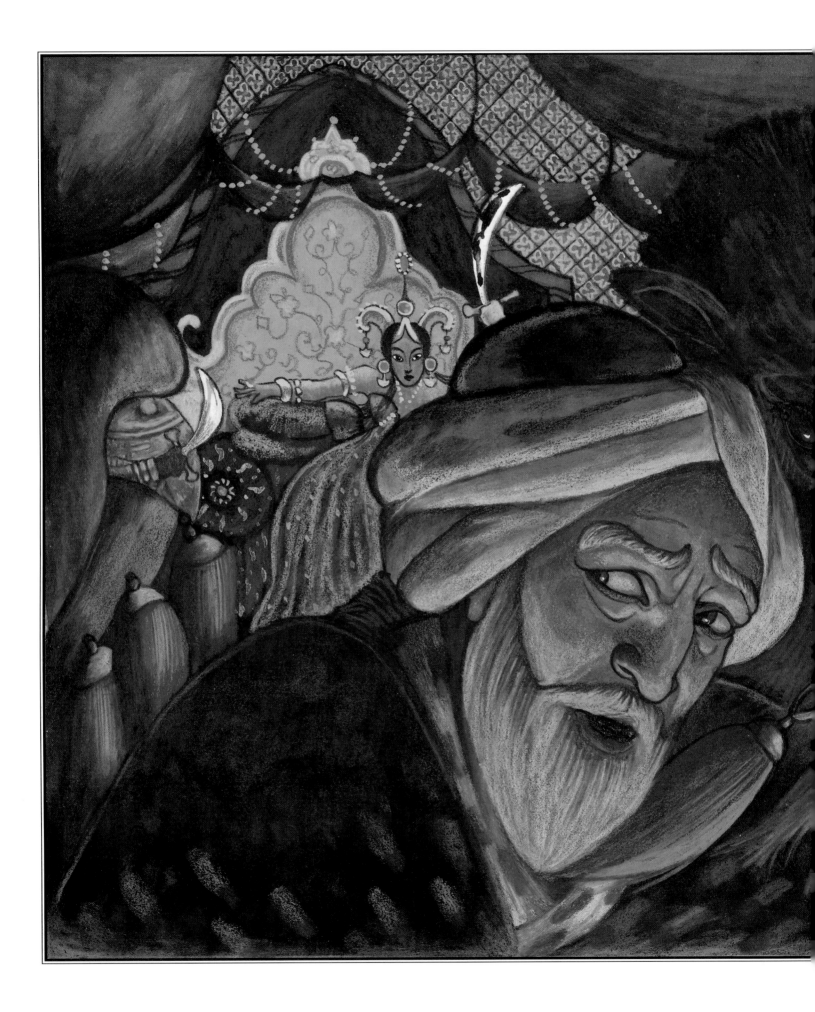

"Quickly! Go! Now!" yelled Musa. And the caravan and all its cavalry flooded out from the gates, which were slowly closing in upon them.

On they rode, full of fear from having seen the lost City of Brass. And they did not stop their travels until they reached the sea.

"Allah be praised!" said the Shakir. "I feel we have survived the worst and that soon our travels will safely end."

And the wise man spoke the truth, for suddenly Musa and Talib and the Shakir were surrounded by a tribe of tall, black men dressed all in hides and burnooses, who greeted them warmly and welcomed them to their homes cut deep into caves facing the sea.

Talib told them of their adventures and why they had come there. Musa gave the King of the black holy people many gifts and jewels, and the King gave them food and drink and many gifts.

"Before you return to your Caliph, then," said the King, "you will want to give him this. One of our fishermen brought it up from the sea."

In his hand was a cucurbit of brass, a bottle stopped with lead, and the seal upon it was that of Solomon, son of David.

After much rejoicing, Musa and Talib and the wise old Shakir turned the caravan around and, taking directions from the King, made their way home.

"And now that we stand before you, great Caliph," said Talib, "and have told you our tale, here is the bottle for which you sent us three years ago!"

The Caliph wiped his hands on his hem and wiped his face with a silk cloth and took the bottle carefully in his hands. No one spoke, and no one moved save the Shakir, who nodded his approval to the Caliph. Then the Caliph slowly turned the lead stopper and pulled it out from the neck of the bottle. A huge, smoky black cloud rose up, high above the canopy of the palace, and with it came a great Jinn of black and gold, and he called out, "Oh, Lord Solomon! I repent! Never again shall I ever do a wicked deed!" And he flew away, far out across the sands, and was gone forever.

"And now, great Caliph," said Talib, "you know what Solomon did with the Jinn of this earth!"

And that is the end of this story as well as of the Jinn!